KT-421-302

N E LINCS LIBRARIES

5 4073 02010453 7

This Faber book belongs to

_____

For Archie
P. J.

For Mia and Lily
L. H.

First published
in the UK in 2019 by
Faber and Faber Limited
Bloomsbury House,
74–77 Great Russell Street,
London WC1B 3DA

Text copyright © Pip Jones, 2019
Illustration copyright
© Laura Hughes, 2019

ISBN 978–0–571–32753–9

All rights reserved.
Printed in Italy

10 9 8 7 6 5 4 3 2 1

The moral rights of Pip Jones
and Laura Hughes
have been asserted.
A CIP record for this book
is available from the British Library.

FABER & FABER has published children's books since 1929. Some of our very first publications included *Old Possum's Book of Practical Cats* by T. S. Eliot starring the now world-famous Macavity, and *The Iron Man* by Ted Hughes. Our catalogue at the time said that 'it is by reading such books that children learn the difference between the shoddy and the genuine'. We still believe in the power of reading to transform children's lives.

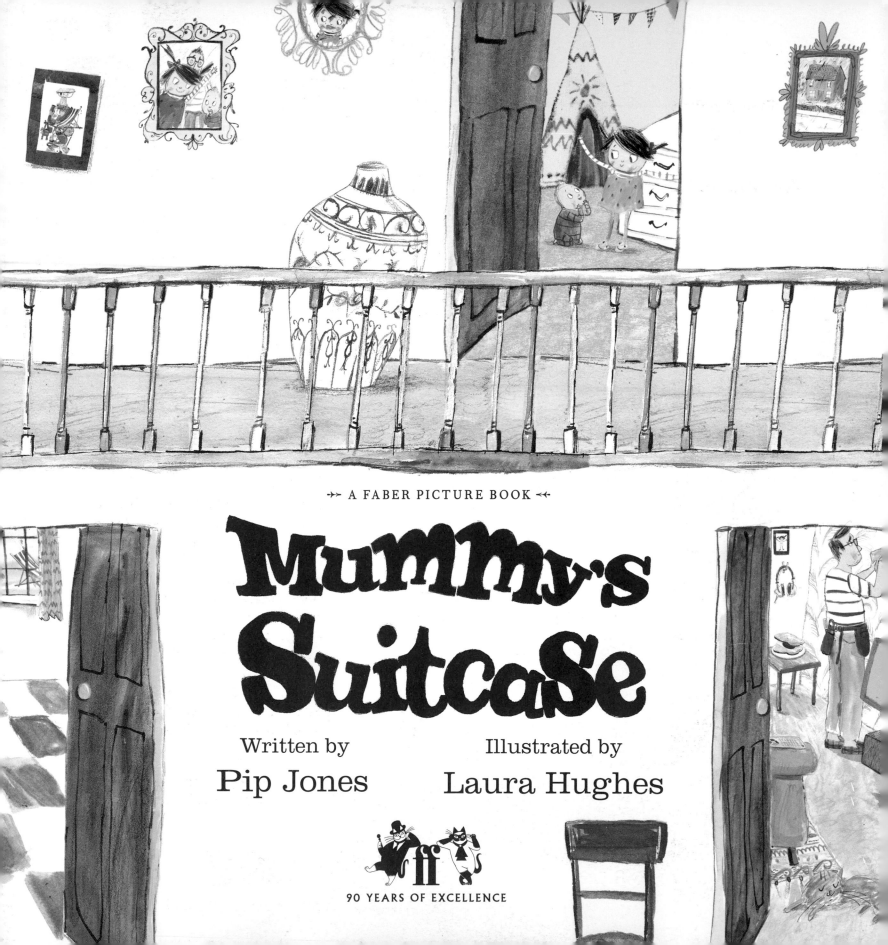

→ A FABER PICTURE BOOK ←

Mummy's Suitcase

Written by

Pip Jones

Illustrated by

Laura Hughes

ff

90 YEARS OF EXCELLENCE

"I'm doing a surprise for you!
No peeking, Mummy. Promise?"

"Promise!"

Poor Mummy has to go away
for *three whole days.*

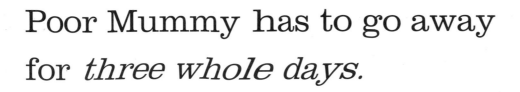

She says she'll miss home VERY much.
I'm going to help her pack!

I need a suitcase . . .
Oh, this will do!

I'll pack the things that Mummy
loves.

Mummy loves Daddy,
so I'll put this lovely photo in.

Mummy loves my bears – she always tucks them in at night.

Mummy loves camping.
Where's the tent? Aha!

Mummy loves a cosy fire.

I'll pack her lots of heavy logs.

Mummy loves counting!
She counts to three **all the time.**

Mummy loves her laptop.
Tip-tap! Tip-tap! *Every day.*

Mummy loves . . .

Hey!

That's not helping, cheeky chops.

Mummy loves these chocolates, which she eats when no one's looking.

But she likes GREENS even better!
She says: "Cabbage is the Best Food Ever!"

Mummy loves her easel,

her fancy pots

and welly boots.

Mummy loves the roses, but I'm not allowed
to pick them, so . . .

Mummy loves the lawnmower

and the hosepipe,

and our pretty pond!

Mummy's packing is nearly done!
I'll just squeeeeeze in her
toothbrush, and . . .

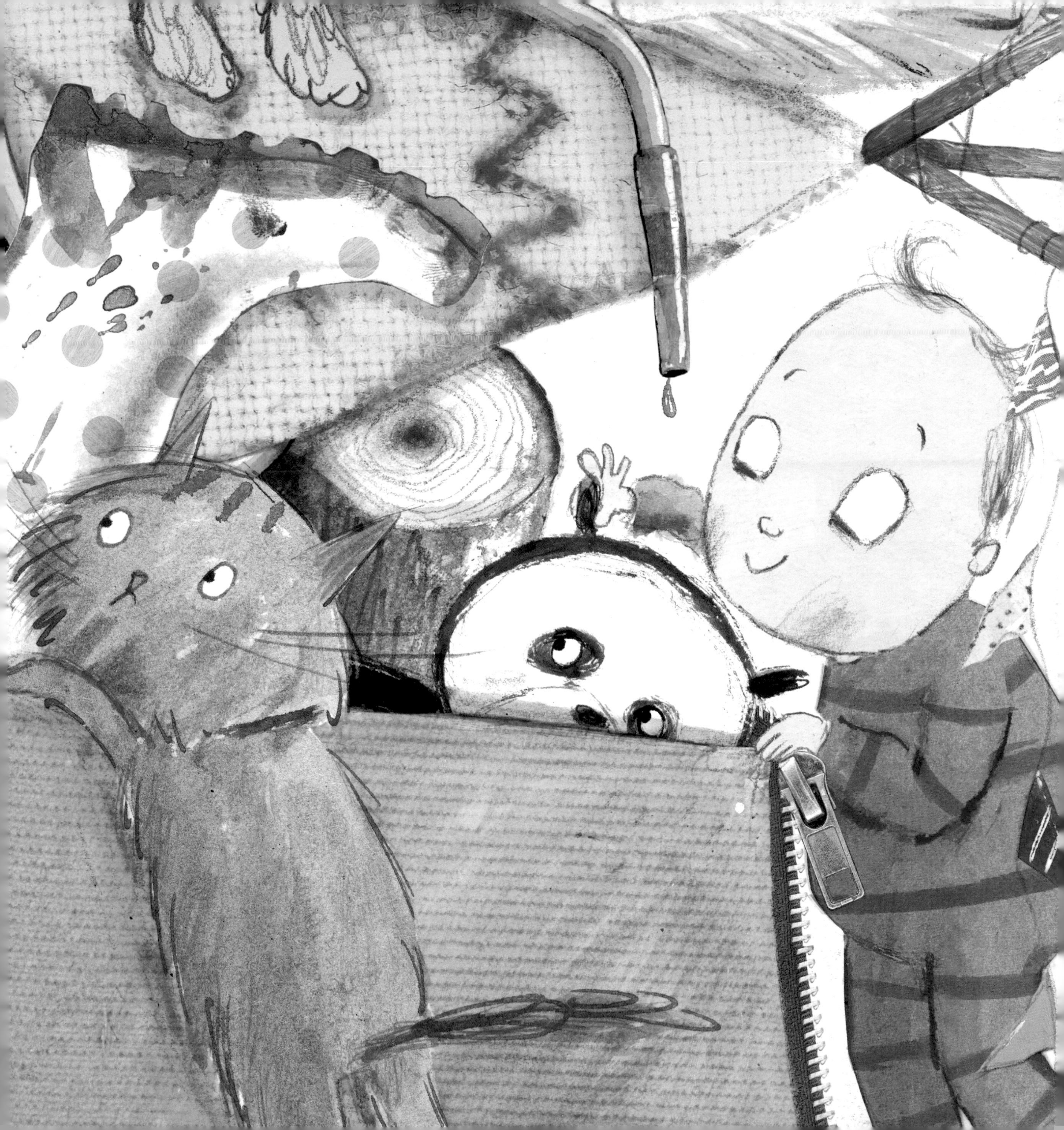

Time to zip the suitcase up.
But I think there's something missing . . .

I know!

More than anything, Mummy loves . . .

Bye-bye, Mummy!
See you soon!